NORTH AMERICA

SOUTH AMERICA

ANTARCTICA

S

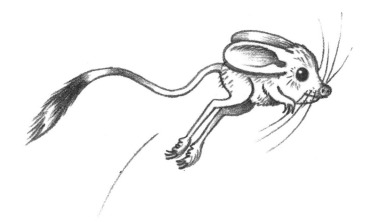

Lena Anlauf & Vitali Konstantinov

GENIUS EARS

A Curious Animal Compendium

Translated from the German
by Marshall Yarbrough

North
South

WHO, WHAT, WHERE?

FENNEC

Vulpes zerda

Fennecs are foxes that live in the sandy deserts of North Africa. During the day they retire into their underground burrows. They are highly playful animals: even the hierarchy in fennec family groups is determined through play. These omnivores use their long ears to listen for prey buried in the sand. Once they've detected their catch, they dig it out.

The fennec is the smallest species of fox, but it has the largest ears relative to its size. The ears account for twenty percent of its body's total surface area and are very flexible.

The function of the fold of skin on the side of each ear can only be guessed at: known as the Henry's pocket, it is thought to help the fennec hear higher pitches and fold its ears.

SQUEAK SQUEEEAK

Fennecs use various sounds to communicate. They can growl or let out a warning bark. Purring signals that the fennec is content, and a squeak means joyful excitement.

This long-eared desert fox is often compared to the short-eared Arctic fox in order to demonstrate Allen's rule, which states that the bodily appendages (legs, ears) of related species are longer in hot and shorter in cold habitats. Having short ears prevents loss of body heat, while having long ears helps an animal cool off, as heat is shed outward over the large surface of the auricle.

Arctic fox

BAT-EARED FOX

Otocyon megalotis

The bat-eared fox lives in semiarid regions and savannahs in eastern and southern Africa. It is the only species of dog that lives almost entirely off insects. Its favorite is termites. Nose to the ground, large ears angled forward, it pads stealthily along, listening out for the slightest sound—it can hear its six-legged prey crawling in their nests. In one year, a bat-eared fox can gobble up more than a million termites.

In the rainy season, bat-eared foxes switch to eating dung beetles and their offspring. They like to hang around hooved animals, where the ground is always teeming with beetles. That's because the beetles eat dung and lay their eggs in it.

The bat-eared fox listens closely for the chewing sound the beetle larvae make as they eat their way out of their dung heap after hatching. With a soft whistle the foxes will summon each other over to a spot where there's food to be found.

GRRRR GRRRRRR

They also communicate through body language: when they feel threatened, they growl, lay their ears flat against their heads, and bristle, causing their fur to stand on end.

LONG-EARED HEDGEHOG

Hemiechinus auritus / Hemiechinus collaris

There are two different species of long-eared hedgehog: the true long-eared hedgehog lives in North Africa, the Middle East, and West and Central Asia, while the darker Indian long-eared hedgehog is found in India and Pakistan.

If they happen to fall, their spines cushion the impact. Sometimes, if they're not too high up, they will drop down on purpose.

These hedgehogs can run, swim, and deftly climb high fences in just a few seconds.

Long-eared hedgehogs are true omnivores: they're happy to eat watermelon, but they also hunt lizards, small snakes, and grasshoppers. They locate their prey with the help of their excellent sense of hearing. Because they're nocturnal, they look for food in the dark, so this comes in especially handy. In dry, hot areas they can survive, if necessary, for a full ten weeks without food or water.

EEEEK
EEEEEK

When a long-eared hedgehog is attacked, it rolls itself up into a ball. As it does so, it folds its long ears forward and covers its eyes to protect them. It can remain in this position for hours if it needs to, waiting until the danger has passed.

Long-eared hedgehogs can communicate using very high-pitched cries that are ultrasonic—they can't be heard by humans. When very agitated, they let out an unexpectedly loud shriek. The little nestlings call their mothers with a shrill whistle.

LONG-EARED JERBOA

Euchoreutes naso

The long-eared jerboa is found in the deserts of southern Mongolia and northern China. Relative to the size of its body, its ears are the largest among all animals known to humans. Although it's a rodent, it feeds for the most part on insects, which it hunts at night.

Individual jerboas' territory can overlap, but in their underground burrows they live alone, or with their young.

The stiff tufts of hair on its toes keep it from sinking into the sand.

Because the jerboa is mostly active at night, it is thought to rely primarily on its hearing while on the hunt. It has been observed listening with its large ears to the sound of insects flying by. When it hears a moth, it can leap up as fast as lightning and catch it in midair.

When it's out hopping around, the long-eared jerboa lays its ears flat on its back to secure them. If the weather is too windy, it prefers to stay in its burrow. It is thought to overwinter there as well, like other species of jerboa.

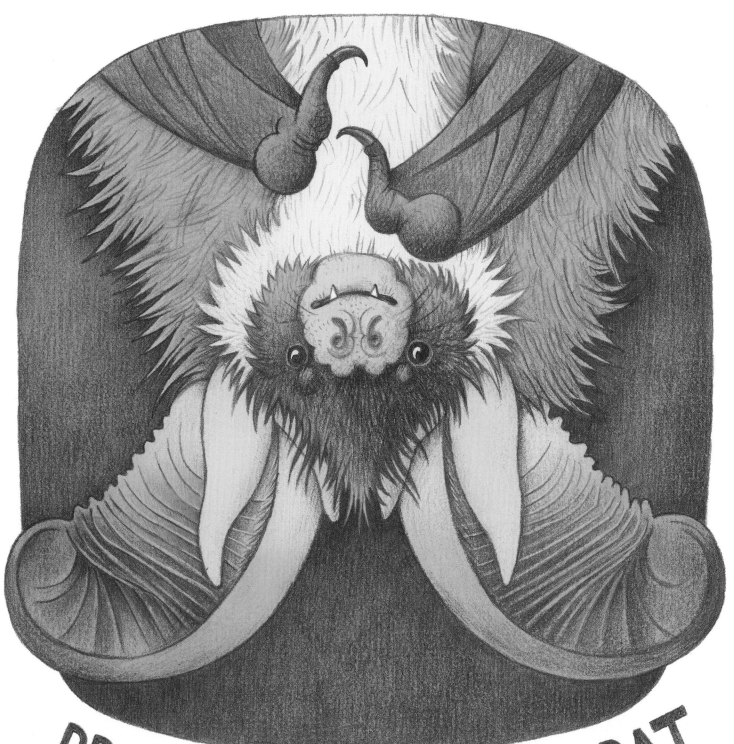

BROWN LONG-EARED BAT

Plecotus auritus

Many bats *see* with their ears: they use echolocation to avoid obstacles and find prey while flying at night. To do this they send out especially high-pitched sounds, which reflect off the objects in front of them and are picked up by their ears. They then use these echoes to form an image of their surroundings. Various species can be found almost everywhere in the world, with ears that come in all sorts of different shapes.

Long-eared myotis

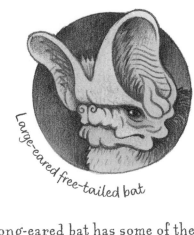

Large-eared free-tailed bat

Round-eared tube-nosed bat

Cuban funnel-eared bat

The European brown long-eared bat has some of the longest ears among bats. By bat standards it's considered a whisperer: in terms of relative volume, its high-pitched, ultrasonic cries are quite soft. And actually, when it's on the hunt, the brown long-eared bat doesn't rely much on echolocation. Its large ears are great for detecting lower-pitched sounds like the soft, telltale rustle of leaves.

The brown long-eared bat listens for the sound of moths' wings as they flutter past.

When it comes to flight speed, this bat's giant ears slow it down somewhat. But it's still an extremely skilled flyer: it can hover in one spot in midair when gathering insects off leaves or the bark of a tree. It can even fly backward.

When brown long-eared bats are at rest, they bend their ears backward. While sleeping and hibernating, they stick their auricles under their wings, so that only the flap of skin that covers them, known as the tragus, is visible.

BLACK-TAILED JACKRABBIT

Lepus californicus

The black-tailed jackrabbit belongs to the genus of true hares. Unlike rabbits, hares are loners. In winter, however, they can gather in groups of up to two hundred fifty individuals for feeding. When this happens, they normally ignore each other, but every now and then they run super fast and chase one another around in a circle.

They are found in the United States and Mexico. Those that live in the hotter south have larger ears than their cousins in the cooler north. They can turn their ears almost all the way around, which enables them to better listen out for suspicious noises and quickly flee if necessary.

When a black-tailed jackrabbit is fleeing from a predator, it constantly changes the way it holds its ears, alternating between four positions: both ears raised, only the left or the right ear raised, or both ears lying flat. The dark tip on the end of each ear is particularly eye-catching, and combined with the ears' continual movement is highly perplexing. When the jackrabbit suddenly makes a sharp turn, the confused predator keeps going straight—and finds itself running the wrong way.

WILD DONKEY

Equus africanus   Equus hemionus   Equus kiang

EEEHH
EEEEHH

Kiang

There are three species of wild donkey. Native to Asia are the onager and the kiang. The African wild donkey, from which all domestic donkeys are descended, lives in Eritrea and Ethiopia. In the wild, it is in acute danger of extinction.

The longest ears among donkeys belong to the African wild donkey. They help it regulate its body temperature in its desert habitat. But this animal also has a keen sense of hearing: for example, it can hear one of its fellow donkeys hee-hawing from several kilometers away.

The sound the kiang makes is different from that of other donkeys: it's a shrill whistle. All donkeys can also grunt, growl, and snort.

You can tell what kind of mood a donkey is in by looking at how it holds its ears.

curious

alert

nervous

tired

enraged

Grévy's zebra

Zedonk

Wild donkey

The legs of the African wild donkey are partially striped and call to mind the legs of a zebra. And in fact, once in a while the African wild donkey will breed with the large-eared Grévy's zebra. The offspring of a zebra stallion and a donkey mare is called a *zedonk*.

GERENUK

Litocranius sclateri / Litocranius walleri

Gerenuks, a type of antelope, live in Somalia, Ethiopia, Kenya, and Tanzania. They make various sounds to communicate with one another: When they're angry, they whistle; in moments of great danger they make a loud bellowing sound. Mother and young speak to one another in soft bleats.

When a gerenuk is alarmed, it keeps its ears still, and either goes completely silent or starts humming softly. Gerenuks aren't the fastest runners, so in this way they hope to go unnoticed.

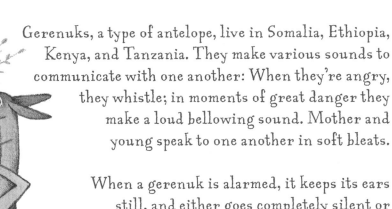

Thanks to their narrow snouts and insensitive lips, gerenuks can munch on leaves that grow on thorny bushes without hurting themselves. The sensitive hairs on their ears also function as an early warning system and help them steer clear of the thorns.

Gerenuks have developed various strategies for getting at food that most other animals in their habitat can't reach: they stand on their hind legs, extend their long necks, and nibble on leaves growing up to two meters (six feet) off the ground.

Bongo

Dik-dik

Other species of African antelope also have large, alert ears for detecting the approach of stealthy predators before it's too late.

Greater kudu

21

Nine-banded armadillo

ARMADILLO

Armadillos live in Central and South America, sometimes underground,
sometimes above. Nine-banded armadillos are also found in North America.
They can barely see and rely mostly on their senses of smell and hearing.

There are twenty different species, with ears shaped all sorts of different ways: tiny ears, flat foldable ears, large funnel-shaped ears, long pointy ears—and lots in between.

Greater fairy armadillo

Brazilian three-banded armadillo

Northern naked-tailed armadillo

Screaming hairy armadillo

Seven-banded armadillo

The Aztec name for the armadillo was *azotochtly*—which can be translated as "tortoise-hare." In Spanish the name for some armadillo species is *mulita*. This is a diminutive form of *muli*, or "mule," a long-eared mix between a horse and a donkey.

Three-banded armadillos can roll themselves up into a ball for protection; they even fold their ears up.

Southern three-banded armadillo

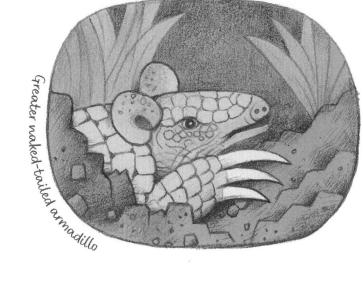

Greater naked-tailed armadillo

The greater naked-tailed armadillo spends a mere ten minutes a day aboveground. The rest of the time it moves around below. It turns its body as it digs; as a result, the entrance to its burrow is nearly perfectly round. While it works, it lays its ears flat, presumably to keep dirt and dust from getting into its ear canals.

23

ELEPHANT
Loxodonta africana

African elephants have the biggest ears in the world: each ear can measure up to two square meters (six square feet)! These giant ears are mainly for climate-control purposes: They are well supplied with blood, so when the elephant flaps its ears, the blood flowing through them gets cooled down by the flow of cool air. When it's cold or raining, the elephant pulls its ears in close to its body.

People have been trying for a long time to figure out the vocal language elephants use for communication. One particular guttural sound has been identified as a call to set out, another as a greeting. When they're very excited, elephants blow a loud trumpet fanfare. But they also communicate through infrasonic cries, which lie below the acoustic range of human hearing. Over small distances they pick up these sounds with their ears; over large distances they detect the resultant ground vibrations with their feet.

Elephants are good at recognizing sounds: the sound of a bee buzzing triggers a spontaneous flight response, complete with a defensive flapping of ears.

Sometimes elephants fan their ears out to their full size in order to make themselves look even bigger and more powerful. They use this trick when fighting among themselves, but it's just as effective as a threatening gesture directed toward other animals and humans.

SERVAL
Leptailurus serval

Servals are small African wildcats that live south of the Sahara in grasslands and savannahs. They have the largest ears of all cat species. When searching for prey, they rely primarily on their excellent sense of hearing.

Unlike lions and cheetahs, which need to lock eyes on their prey in order to hunt, servals like to go hunting in tall grass. They creep forward carefully on their long legs and sometimes stand motionless for up to fifteen minutes, listening for noises that reveal the presence of prey nearby. They can pinpoint the location of even the softest rustling sound, and silently ready themselves to pounce from more than three meters (nine feet) away.

Very rarely, a serval will have completely black fur. This phenomenon is called melanism.

The fur on the back of the serval's ears is arranged in a pattern that resembles an eye. These eyespots probably function as a way of scaring other animals off.

PAINTED DOG
Lycaon pictus

Painted dogs (also called African wild dogs) live in savannah regions throughout the African continent. At present the largest population is found in Tanzania. At one time they lived together in packs of up to one hundred; today it's usually no more than twenty. They are in danger of going extinct.

When a painted dog loses its way, it makes a noise that sounds like *hoo-hoo*— it's hoping that the pack will answer, and it can find its way back. Happy dogs communicate with surprisingly high-pitched chirping noises. Body language also comes into play, particularly the way the dogs hold their ears.

dominant

submissive

CHEEP

Every pack has an alpha male and alpha female. Together the whole pack looks after the alpha pair's offspring. Painted dogs are very nurturing: in addition to providing for their own young, they also provide food for injured and old dogs.

An interesting method of communication has been observed among painted dogs in Botswana: the pack votes by sneezing whether to set out for the hunt. A sneeze means *yes*, silence *no*. The voices of the alpha dogs count a bit more, but nevertheless, the decision to move out or stay put is always made communally.

Mohol bush baby

GALAGO

Galagos, or bush babies, are primates that live on the African continent south of the Sahara.
Their family is comprised of six genera, which altogether contain twenty different species.
Scientists suspect, however, that there are significantly more species that have yet to be discovered.

Western dwarf galago

Eastern dwarf galago

Lesser bush baby

Needle-clawed bush baby

Squirrel galago

Greater galago

Galago genera

You can tell different types of galago apart by the color of their fur, the slightly differing shapes of their ears, and the distinct sounds they make.

Every species of galago has highly flexible ears that can bend backward. Folding their ears together lets galagos sleep more peacefully. If their ears lie flat, however, this can signal excitement of either the fearful or the cheerful kind: you see it when they feel threatened, for example, or when two galagos greet each other, briefly touching noses.

Specially structured muscles in their legs enable them to jump more than two meters (six feet):

This way they can move lightning-fast.

The galago's sense of hearing is very important for hunting: it can hear insects in the dark and even snatch them out of midair as they fly past.

Large-eared greater galago

UHWAH
UH
WAH

Galagos squeak, bark, and chirp to communicate with one another. They can also let out a shrill whistle that lets all the other galagos nearby know where exactly a looming threat is to be found. Every species of galago has its own highly distinct cries. The cries of some sound like the crying of a human child. This is where they get the name *bush baby*.

31

AYE-AYE
Daubentonia madagascariensis

Aye-ayes make their home on Madagascar. During the day they sleep in meticulously woven nests high up in the trees, more than twenty meters (sixty feet) off the ground. The large ears of these otherwise shaggy-haired primates are hairless and somewhat furrowed. This helps form the ears into a bowl shape, which increases their sensitivity to sound. Baby aye-ayes are usually floppy-eared.

The primates talk to each other by making various noises:

GGNOFF GGNOFF

A grunt or hiss indicates a threat, while a sneeze-like sound means great danger. To show affection they make a loving *ggnoff* sound.

The aye-aye is an omnivore: it munches on fruit and mushrooms, uses its long middle finger to scoop nectar out of flower blossoms, and particularly likes eating insect larvae. When searching for them it uses a knocking technique. The aye-aye can heat up its extraordinarily long finger by up to 6° Celsius (around 11° Fahrenheit), which makes it even more flexible and sensitive. The aye-aye knocks on the bark of rotten tree trunks, very fast, up to eight times per second. As it knocks, it listens closely to the sound and can hear if there are any hollow spots with maggots hiding inside.

Aye-ayes give many people the creeps. There are several folktales about them. This fear might stem from these intelligent animals' unusual curiosity and lack of timidity: Researchers have given accounts of aye-ayes appearing out of nowhere and approaching to sniff them.

GREATER GLIDER

Petauroides minor

Petauroides

Petauroides armillatus

volans

Greater gliders are found in Australian eucalyptus forests. It wasn't until 2020 that scientists confirmed that they are divided into three distinct species. When this discovery was announced and the photo of a glider appeared in the news, many thought it was a joke—the fuzzy-eared animal looked too cute to be true.

The glider's long, soft fur comes in different colors: gray, white, dark brown, or a mix. The fur also covers the backs of its giant ears, making the ears look even more impressive. Gliders can glide for distances of up to one hundred meters (three hundred feet).

In order to replace the tree hollows that the gliders are losing as a result of forest fires and deforestation, conservationists are putting up nesting boxes, built just for gliders. These boxes offer them protection from heat and cold.

Greater gliders live off eucalyptus leaves and buds. Because this diet isn't exactly high in calories, they sleep through most of the day, alternating between as many as twenty different sleeping hollows, some of which are way up high in the treetops.

Greater gliders are extremely quiet animals. They almost never utter any sort of cry. This sets them apart from other large-eared marsupials in their habitat: in contrast, the highly varied cries of the yellow-bellied glider fill the Australian forest and can be heard up to half a kilometer (almost a third of a mile) away.

HIAR-HIAR

CHRL-CHRRL

SCHROO-SCHROO

Yellow-bellied glider

TUFT-EARED

CARACAL & LYNX

The caracal can be found across broad swaths of Africa and Asia. Its name comes from Turkish and means "black ear." Thanks to its tufted ears it bears a resemblance to the lynx, which is native to Europe, North America, and Asia; indeed, the caracal is sometimes called the desert lynx. To this day there is disagreement among researchers as to what the brush-like tufts of fur on its ears are for. There are various theories. The first is that the tufts are supposed to imitate blades of grass swaying in the wind. The second is that the fine tufts of fur help channel sound into the inner ear. Finally, the third theory posits that they help them communicate with fellow caracals. There are similar theories about the lynx's ears: It's said that the tufts help the lynx determine which way the wind is blowing. Knowing this, it can lie in wait facing windward, so that its scent doesn't warn its prey.

Caracal caracal

Lynx lynx

DWARF BUFFALO

Dwarf buffaloes, or African forest buffaloes, are the smallest species of African buffalo. What makes their long ears distinctive are the three-colored tassels that adorn them. These tassels turn their ears into impressive flyswatters, which come in handy for shooing away pesky insects.

Syncerus nanus

BINTURONG

The binturong is found in the rain forests of Southeast Asia. The impressive tufts of fur on its ears are longer than the ears themselves. When they're in a cheerful mood, binturongs make a giggling sound, but they can also growl, grunt, and hiss. Another unique characteristic is their odor: they smell like popcorn.

Arctictis binturong

RED RIVER HOG

Red river hogs live in West and Central Africa and on Madagascar. The tufts of hair on their ears—more than ten centimeters (four inches) long—help them intimidate other animals: when a red river hog feels threatened, the hair on its ears sticks out to the side, while the ridge of hair along its spine stands on end. This makes the hog look significantly bigger.

Potamochoerus porcus

SQUIRREL

There are about 280 different squirrel species worldwide. With the exception of Australia, Madagascar, and Antarctica, squirrels have conquered nearly every habitat. In the cold winter, the Eurasian red squirrel grows warm tufts of fur on its ears. In the forests of Borneo, on the other hand, you can find squirrels whose ears are tufted all year round, such as the tiny, moss-eating tufted pygmy squirrel—but they haven't yet been studied very much.

Exilisciurus whiteheadi

Sciurus vulgaris

MARMOSETS

Golden-white tassel-ear marmoset

Golden-white bare-ear marmoset

Golden-handed tamarin

White-tufted-ear marmoset

Cotton-top tamarin

Tufted-ear marmoset

Pied tamarin

The tamarins and marmosets that make up the Callitrichidae family all have impressive ears: among the approximately fifty different species, some have ears that stick out, naked and goblin-like, some have ears ringed by a fan of fur, and still others have ears overgrown with fluffy tufts of hair.

These South American monkeys use birdlike chirping sounds to communicate among themselves in their family groups, which are of great importance to them. But the white-tufted-ear marmoset also uses its ears to communicate in a different fashion: If the tufts of fur on its ears stand on end and it's also furrowing its brow or staring with its eyes narrowed, that means it's angry. Tufts flattened against its head are a sign of fear.

TSREE-TSRREEE

TSE-TSE TSE-TSE-TSE

A composer in the United States wrote music for marmosets and recorded the music on cello. One piece sounds like cheerful monkey noises, the other like noises of fright. After hearing the spooky song, the monkeys became uneasy. The pleasant song, on the other hand, had a relaxing effect on them. To human ears, both compositions sound extremely bizarre.

When a margay is trying to make a meal of a pied tamarin, the monkey's ears can be its undoing. From its hiding place the predator imitates the calls of tamarin young in order to lure the monkey out of its tree. But the tamarin's hearing is often good enough to catch the deception in time.

MI-MI MI-MI-MI

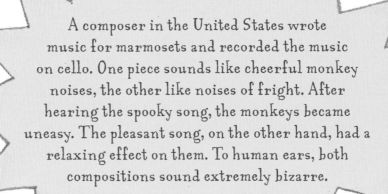

HONEY BADGER

Mellivora capensis

The honey badger can be found across large swaths of Africa and Asia. It is one of the few mammals without external ears: its ears are completely covered by its thick skin, with only their edges visible, outlining the entrance to the ear canal. This way when the honey badger gets into a fight, its enemies don't have any vulnerable area to attack. The honey badger is considered an exceptionally fearless animal; despite its diminutive size, it will pick a fight with leopards, lions, and buffaloes.

The honey badger's entire body is built for fighting. It has long claws and sharp teeth. No animal can bite through its extremely thick skin, which hangs off its body like a loose coat.

If a lion tries to grab it, it will slip right out of its paws. It can let out a frightening grunting sound or a rattling roar. But mothers and their young communicate with one another by purring.

The honey badger loves honey and bee larvae! When raiding a nest, it shuts the folds of its ears to protect its sensitive ear canals from insect stings.

Baby cheetahs bear a resemblance to honey badgers. It is believed that the coloring of their fur developed this way to have an intimidating effect on other animals.

SOMETIMES RED-EARED

TASMANIAN DEVIL

The Tasmanian devil gets its name in part from a conspicuous feature of its ears: when the animal is agitated, or quarreling with others of its species, its blood pressure shoots up and causes its ears to turn beet red.

UUAAAH
AAAHHHH
UUUÄÄÄHH

Sarcophilus harrisii

The Tasmanian devil can't see particularly well, and so it relies on its senses of smell and hearing. Hearing also plays an important role in communication: Tasmanian devils can let out an incredibly loud screech, and they also snort, cough, grunt, and growl, mainly to warn other Tasmanian devils to keep away from their food. Sneezing is also thought to serve intimidation purposes.

BLACK RAT

Rats have an unbelievably keen sense of hearing; they can even perceive ultrasounds. But their hearing organs have yet another, quite remarkable feature: researchers have discovered that rats smile with their ears. When they're happy, their ears lie closer to their body and turn pinkish-red from increased blood flow. Furthermore, if you tickle a rat, it can make laughing sounds. These are so high-pitched, however, that humans can't hear them.

Rattus rattus

HUMAN

Homo sapiens

Human ears can also reveal their owners' emotions: If a person is worked up, extremely angry, or particularly embarrassed about something, their auricles can turn beet red. When this happens, the ears feel very hot to the touch, thanks to the strong flow of blood. The effect subsides on its own once the person calms down. They say that people who blush can be forgiven more quickly.

FAUX-EARED

Some chameleon species, such as the elephant-eared chameleon and the Meller's chameleon, seem to have giant ears. What look like auditory organs, however, are merely flaps of skin, which the animal can raise in order to impress others, whether it's looking for a mate or facing a potential threat. Chameleons don't actually have external ears, and with their inner ears they can barely hear a thing. They rely mostly on their eyes.

Trioceros melleri

LONG-EARED OWL

Asio otus

About half of all owl species possess distinct ear-like feathers. The long-eared owl is even named after them. The exact function of the feathery tufts is unknown, although they can indicate the owl's mood. What's certain is that they have nothing to do with its magnificent sense of hearing: for that purpose, the owl has long, slit-shaped ear openings located at somewhat different heights on either side of its head. The owl's facial disc helps pick up sound waves and channel them into the ear openings. As for the owl itself, thanks to its remarkable feathers it moves almost without a sound.

44

DUMBO OCTOPUS

Dumbo octopuses live in the deep sea, up to 5,000 meters (15,000 feet) below the ocean's surface. What seem to be giant ears on their heads are actually fins. They flutter this way and that when the octopus swims, calling to mind Disney's Dumbo, the flying elephant, after whom this sea creature was named. The fist-sized octopuses of related genera are also sometimes informally called Dumbos. There is much research still to be done on all of them.

Grimpoteuthis imperator

Opisthoteuthis californiana

FILE-EARED TREE FROG

File-eared tree frogs look like they have little ears sticking up out of their heads. This appearance is deceiving, but their actual ears are in fact located, quite unassumingly, right below the false ones. Other frogs detect sound waves with their mouths. Some have inner ears that are so specialized that they can only hear the croaking of their own species.

Polypedates otilophus

EARED LEAFHOPPER

Ledra aurita

Name and appearance are also misleading in the case of the eared leafhopper: it is an insect, and no insect has actual auricles. It can still hear, though: leaf-hopper ears are located on the insect's rear end. As for other insects, crickets have hearing organs on their knees, and mosquitos hear with their antennae.

GLOSSARY

Acoustic range: The range of frequencies within which a living thing can perceive a cry or a noise. For humans it lies between 16 hertz and 20,000 hertz, approximately. One hertz (Hz) equals one oscillation (vibration) per second. If the number in hertz is low, the sound is perceived as low-pitched; if the number is high, the sound is heard as high-pitched. Many animals have a greater hearing range than humans and can hear and even produce ultrasounds or infrasounds. (–> *Illustration, p. 48*)

Allen's rule: Formulated in 1877 by the American zoologist Joel Asaph Allen, Allen's rule states in part that among related species of mammals, bodily appendages (for example, ears) will be proportionally shorter in colder climates than in warmer climates. This doesn't hold true for all animals, of course, but it does apply to hedgehogs, hares, foxes, and elephants.

Alpha: The top animal, leader of a pack or a herd.

Auricle: The external, visible part of the ear. (–> *Illustration, p. 49*)

Binomial nomenclature (Latin species names): This naming system, invented in the eighteenth century by the Swedish naturalist Carl Linnaeus, is used all over the world and avoids misunderstandings between people who speak different languages. The binomial name of an animal species is written in Latin and made up of two parts: first comes the name of the genus, and after that the name of the species. If there is a third name, it refers to the subspecies. Whoever first documents a species for the scientific community gets to choose a name, though they have to follow certain international rules. Only in a few exceptional cases can a binomial name be changed later. Incidentally, the name is not always derived from Latin; names are also frequently derived from Greek. Often you can identify an animal's traits by looking at its name: the Painted dog (African wild dog), for example, is called *Lycaon pictus*; the word *pictus* can be translated roughly as "colorfully painted," referring to the coloration of its fur. Other names describe where the animal lives: the aye-aye of Madagascar is called *Daubentonia madagascariensis*.

Communication: The exchange of information between two or more living things, which can occur in any number of ways (cries, movements of the body, odors, and so on).

Cry: A sound or noise that an animal or human makes vocally.

Desert: An area of land with few or no plants. Deserts usually occur due to cold or lack of water. The largest desert in the world is a cold desert: Antarctica. The second and third largest are arid deserts: the Sahara in Africa and the Gobi in Asia. Animals that live in deserts must adapt to the extreme living conditions: examples of such adaptations are the large ears of the fennec, the long-eared jerboa, and the long-eared hedgehog, which help regulate the animals' body temperature.

Ear: Often used interchangeably with *auricle* to refer to the exterior portion of our hearing organ. This sensory organ allows us to hear sound.

Ear canal: The ear has an inner auditory canal and an outer auditory canal. The outer auditory canal (also called the ear canal) channels sound from the auricle to the eardrum. The inner auditory canal (or inner auditory meatus) provides a pathway for the auditory vestibular nerve, which controls hearing and balance and extends into the inner ear. (—> *Illustration, p. 49*)

Echolocation: An echo occurs when sound waves hit an obstacle and bounce back. The echo of an initial sound always remains at the same pitch; only the volume is lower. Some animals, like the bat (and underwater animals like whales and dolphins, along with some rodents, researchers believe) form a picture of their surroundings by detecting and interpreting echoes—they use echolocation. People can also learn to do this, to an extent.

Eyespot: A marking on the fur or body of an animal that resembles an eye. On prey animals it mostly serves to ward off predators. On predators, like the serval, the eyespot on the ear is thought to have an additional function: making it easier for the young to follow their mother.

Facial disc: The distinctly shaped formation of feathers on the face of an owl or other type of bird. The formation amplifies sound waves and directs them toward the ear canal.

Floppy ears: Some animals have ears that lie flat or are bent at certain times—for example, when they're babies or when they want to get some sleep.

Permanently floppy ears, however, are a trait found exclusively among domesticated animals.

Genus (plural: genera): A category or group that includes more than one species.

Glide: A flight through the air that begins with a leap and relies on the use of gliding membranes (thin stretches of skin that can be spread out between body parts) to substantially lengthen the time aloft. A gliding animal can also change directions mid-glide: greater gliders, for example, move in this fashion from tree to tree. Fun fact: When preparing for flight, the greater glider has to hold its front paws under its face, which makes it look particularly cute. It does this because, unlike other gliding animals, its membranes don't extend all the way to its paws, but rather just to its elbows.

Hearing: The ability to perceive sound. The auricles help pick up sound waves and channel them into the auditory canal. There the waves hit the eardrum, a thin membrane that begins to vibrate and passes the signal on to the ossicles, the tiny bones of the middle ear. These amplify the vibrations and direct them to the cochlea. In the cochlea are the sensory cells that convert the vibrations into electric signals and pass them on to the brain via the auditory nerve.

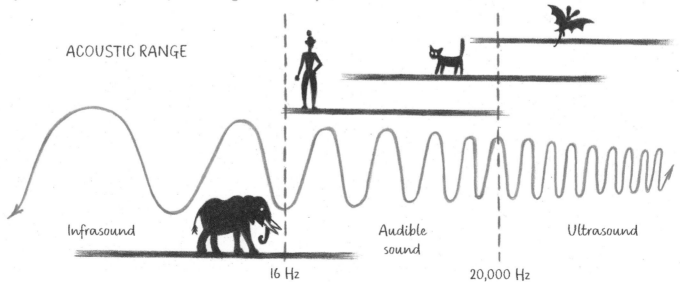

ACOUSTIC RANGE

Infrasound   Audible sound   Ultrasound

16 Hz   20,000 Hz

Heat regulation: Lowering of the body's temperature or shedding of body heat to prevent overheating. This is part of the process of thermoregulation undergone by warm-blooded animals. Most animals have developed adaptations or strategies, suited to their habitats, that enable them to protect their bodies from getting too hot or too cold. The large ears of an African elephant, well supplied with blood, are one example.

Henry's pocket: A fold of skin that's found on all cat ears, some dog ears, bat ears, and the ears of a few other animals. Its function is unknown, but it might help the animal hear particularly high pitches and might increase the flexibility of the ear. (–> *Illustration below*)

Infrasonic: See "Sound"

Locate: To find out where something is.

Mammals (class): As a rule, a mammal is an animal that gives birth to live young and then nurses them. There are, however, a few exceptions, like the egg-laying echidna.

Marsupial (infraclass): A mammal that is born alive but must first develop further in its mother's pouch until it reaches viability. Greater gliders and Tasmanian devils are marsupials.

Melanism: A phenomenon that results in animals that are completely black, in contrast to the usual coloring of their species. The most well-known instances of melanism are panthers (black leopards or jaguars), but this anomaly can occur among other species as well (like the serval).

Nestling: A young animal that still lives in its parents' nest and is dependent on them for food.

Omnivore: An animal whose diet consists of a mix of plants and animals.

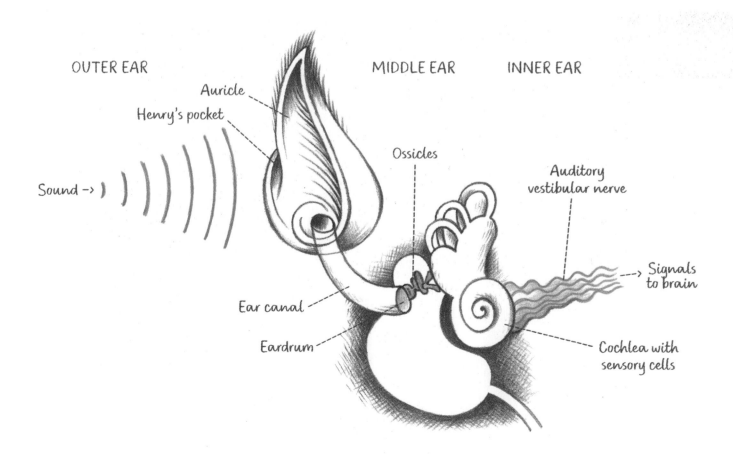

OUTER EAR   MIDDLE EAR   INNER EAR

Auricle

Henry's pocket

Ossicles

Auditory vestibular nerve

Sound –>

Signals to brain

Ear canal

Eardrum

Cochlea with sensory cells

Organ: Part of the body that performs a certain function (or several). The ear as the auditory organ is one example.

Pack: A group of mammals in which all the members know one another and each individual usually has a specific role.

Predator: An animal whose diet consists of other animals.

Prey: An animal that is hunted and eaten by a predator. Termites are prey animals; from their perspective the bat-eared fox is a predator. At the same time, however, the bat-eared fox is prey to larger predators.

Sound: Something that can be heard. We humans only hear sound within a certain range. Extremely high pitches that are beyond our hearing are called ultrasounds. Bats can hear ultrasonic pitches and use their echoes to find their way around. Extremely low pitches that are beyond our hearing are called infrasounds. Some animals can perceive infrasounds from over one hundred kilometers (sixty-two miles) away. Depending on how sounds are perceived, they can be described as loud or soft. These descriptions can vary considerably, depending on who is hearing what. A sound that one species of animal with sensitive hearing hears as loud can to another animal be soft or not audible at all. Low-pitched sounds are felt to be softer than higher-pitched sounds of the same sonic intensity. Generally speaking, however, it can be said that intense oscillations (vibrations) produce loud sounds and weak oscillations produce soft sounds. (–> *Illustration, p. 48*)

Sound waves: Invisible vibrations, for example those made by air or water particles. When organs (such as vocal cords) or things (like the strings of a ukulele) vibrate, they create a wave.

The vibrations spread to the air or water particles, which collide with other particles. Sound waves are the result. The study of sound is called acoustics.

Species: Animals that belong to the same species exhibit a multitude of shared traits and can only reproduce with each other. There are, however, exceptions to this second rule. When two different species interbreed, their offspring are called hybrids. Often in science there is disagreement, and the way animals are classified is continually updated as more is found out about them. As a result, the names for different species are sometimes confusing: honey badgers, for example, aren't really badgers at all. Each species belongs to a larger genus, which in turn belongs to a larger family. Several families make up an order, several orders are in a class, and so on. The farther out you go, the fewer traits the animals have in common with each other, until finally you get to a kingdom. For example, the animal kingdom is made up of every animal.

Tassel: A tufted bundle of threads or hairs.

Tragus: A flap of skin covering the ear that some animals, like bats, can control independently using muscle movement. We humans also have a tragus on each ear—but we have to use a finger to close it over the opening of our ear canal.

Tufted ear: An auricle that is covered in or surrounded by tufts of hair.

Ultrasonic: –> *Sound*

SOURCES AND NOTES

The information in this book is drawn from various sources, including *The Handbook of the Mammals of the World* edited by Don Ellis Wilson and Russel Mittermeier (nine volumes, 2009 2019), *The Mammals of the Southern African Subregion* by J. D. Skinner and Christian T. Chimimba (2005), and *Bats: An Illustrated Guide to All Species* by Marianne Taylor (2019). In addition, some pages include references to specific study results, which are listed below.

World Map

The map at the very front of the book is modeled on the AuthaGraph world map developed by the Japanese architect Hajime Narukawa, currently the most accurate representation of the earth's land masses and bodies of water. Narukawa came up with his map because the well-known depiction of the earth based on Gerhard Mercator's rendering from the sixteenth century is far removed from reality. Because the earth is spherical (or close to it), its image appears distorted on a flat map: in the Mercator projection, Greenland, for example, appears to be about the same size as Africa, even though the continent is in fact almost fourteen times bigger than the island.

Page 17: "Ear Flashing Behavior of Black-tailed Jackrabbits (*Lepus californicus*)" (Kamler/Ballard, 2006).

Page 19: "A mysterious zebra-donkey hybrid (zedonk or zonkey) produced under natural mating: A case report from Borana, southern Ethiopia" (Megersa/Biffa/Kumsa, 2006).

Page 23: The armadillo drawing in the middle of the page was inspired by Central American art.

Page 29: "Sneeze to leave: African wild dogs (*Lycaon pictus*) use variable quorum thresholds facilitated by sneezes in collective decisions" (Walker et al., 2017)

Page 39: The tamarin music was composed and recorded in 2009 by the cellist David Teie of the University of Maryland, College Park, who cooperated with psychologist Charles T. Snowdon of the University of Wisconsin-Madison, who supplied the recordings and research that informed the composition. "Affective responses in tamarins elicited by species-specific music" (Snowdon/Teie, 2009)

"Hunting Strategy of the Margay (*Leopardus wiedii*) to Attract the Wild Pied Tamarin (*Saguinus bicolor*)" (Calleia/Rohe/Gordo, 2009)

Page 41: "A Possible Case of Mimicry in Larger Mammals" (Eaton, 1976)

Page 43: "Facial Indicators of Positive Emotions in Rats" (Finlayson et al., 2016)

"Laughing Rats? Playful Tickling Arouses High-Frequency Ultrasonic Chirping in Young Rodents" (Panksepp/Burgdorf, 2010)

"Saved by the blush: Being trusted despite defecting" (Dijk/Koenig/Ketelaar/de Jong, 2011)

Page 46, bonus animal: Here you'll find a Western pygmy possum. It lives in forested areas in Australia. Its favorite foods are nectar and pollen, and when it eats, it helps pollinate flowers. When the weather gets too cold and uncomfortable for it, it falls into a sleep-like state, protectively curling up its large oval ears and folding them down over its head.

INDEX

LENA ANLAUF was born in the Ruhr region of Germany. She studied book studies and philosophy in Mainz and Leiden and completed a further education course on pedagogy of literacy and literature as well as a remote course on children's and young adult literature at the STUBE in Vienna. Today she lives in Marburg, works as editorial director at the kunstanstifter verlag, researches historical picture books, writes and designs her own book projects, and puts on workshops for children.

VITALI KONSTANTINOV was born in Ukraine. He studied architecture and art and has taught illustration courses at universities in several countries as well as numerous workshops for children. His work has been exhibited extensively, has received many prizes, and has been published in forty different countries. Today Vitali works as a freelance illustrator and author and lives in Marburg. He drew the illustrations for *Genius Ears* with drawing ink and colored pencil on watercolor paper.

GENIUS NOSES
A Curious Animal Compendium

An illustrated collection about animal noses and their amazing functions! Early STEM has never been more fun. Everything kids ever wanted to know about animal noses around the world!

This special collection of animals takes us around the globe and amazes us with the curious diversity of nature. Whether it's the aardvark, the elephant, the pig, or the saiga antelope, they all have wonderful noses. In addition to a wide array of functions, noses tell us a lot about animal habits and habitats.

Author Lena Anlauf has compiled the most exciting facts and stories about noses from the animal kingdom, while illustrator Vitali Konstantinov introduces us to the individual animals in impressive portraits—with wit and attention to detail.

Which animal can smell underwater? Which one uses its nose as a snorkel? What can animals do with their noses besides smell? Readers will find these answers and more in this entertaining collection filled with surprising and unusual facts.

ISBN: 978-0-7358-4535-0

"Readers can dip in and out for a plethora of engaging and even silly facts."
Booklist

"Genius Noses is a winner for older kids. Five stars out of five."
NY Journal of Books

"A Eureka! nonfiction honor book"
California Reading Association

First published in the United States, Great Britain, Canada,
Australia, and New Zealand in 2024 by NorthSouth Books Inc.,
an imprint of NordSüd Verlag AG, CH-8050 Zürich, Switzerland.

Distributed in the United States by NorthSouth Books, Inc., New York 10016.
Library of Congress Cataloging-in-Publication Data is available.
ISBN: 978-0-7358-4562-6 (trade edition)
1 3 5 7 9 • 10 8 6 4 2
Printed in Latvia
www.northsouth.com